CHRISTMAS LULLABY

by NANCY JEWELL
Illustrated by STEFANO VITALE

Clarion Books / *New York*

a Houghton Mifflin Company imprint
215 Park Avenue South, New York, NY 10003
Text copyright © 1994 by Nancy Jewell
Illustrations copyright © 1994 by Stefano Vitale

The illustrations for this book were executed in oil paint on wooden panels.
The text was set in 19 pt. Goudy

Printed in the USA

Library of Congress Cataloging-in-Publication Data

Jewell, Nancy.
    Christmas lullaby / by Nancy Jewell ; illustrated by Stefano Vitale.
            p.   cm.
    Summary: A story in rhyme about the animals that attended the
Baby Jesus.
    ISBN 0-395-66586-8
    1. Jesus Christ—Nativity—Juvenile fiction.   [1. Jesus Christ—
Nativity—Fiction. 2. Animals—Fiction. 3. Stories in rhyme.]   I.   Vitale,
Stefano, ill.   II. Title.
PZ8.3.J47Ch   1994
[E]—dc20   93-38786
                                                    CIP
                                                    AC

BP 10 9 8 7 6 5 4 3 2 1

For Granny and Grandpa Royes
—N.J.

To Anna
—S.V.

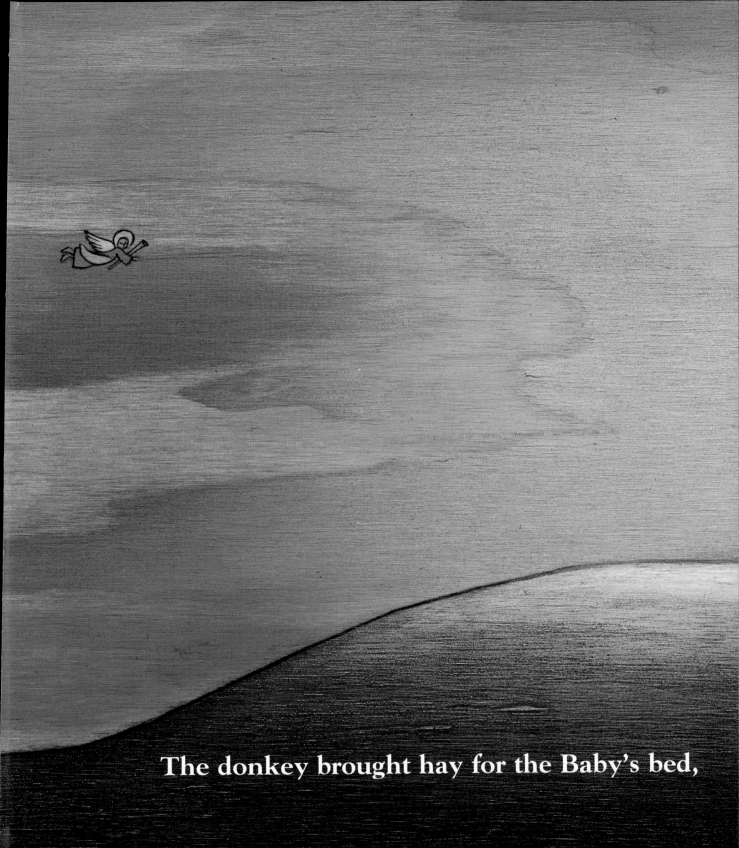

The donkey brought hay for the Baby's bed,

the lamb brought fleece to pillow His head.

The cow gave the Baby a drink of her milk,

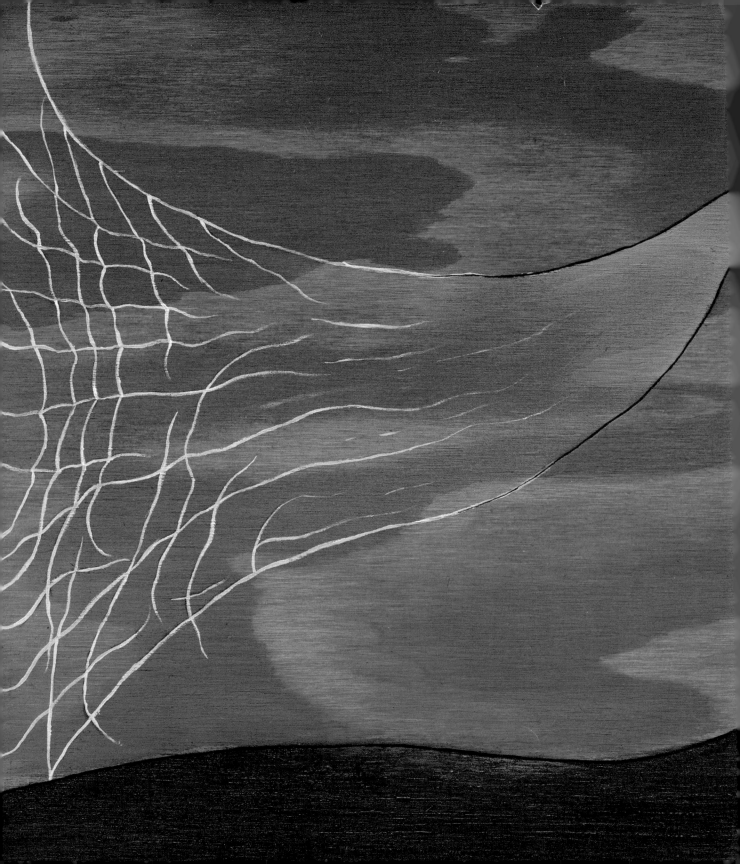

the spider a blanket she spun from fine silk.

The raven brought Him a bright shiny bead,

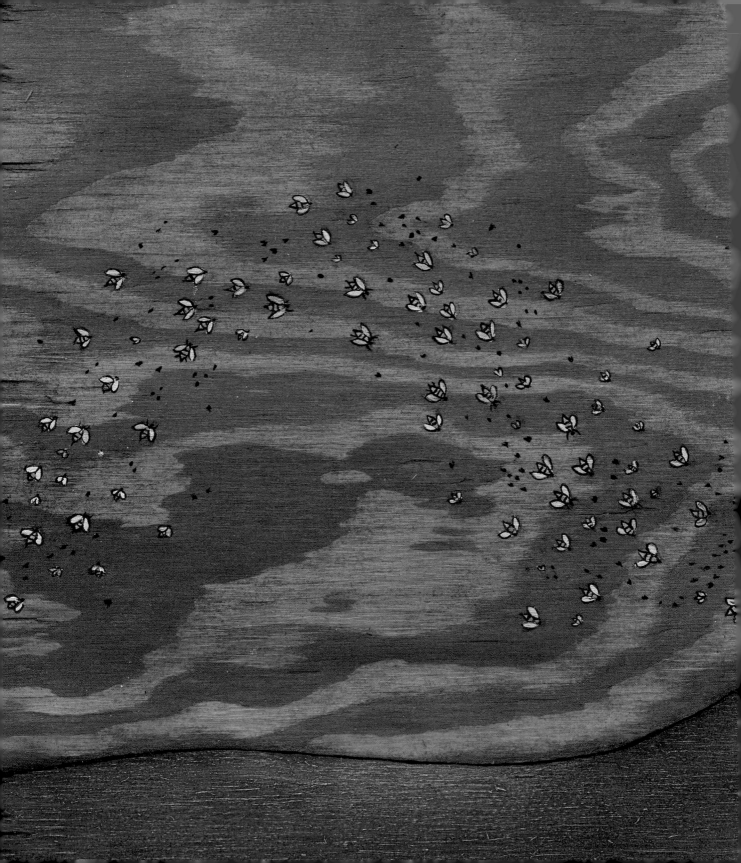

the bees brought honey, the sparrow a seed.

The mouse gave the Baby grass from her nest,

the dove a feather she plucked from her breast.

Then, to a chorus of moos, baas, and peeps,

the cat and her kittens purred Him to sleep.